# You can't Catch Me

*by Charlotte Doyle • pictures by Rosanne Litzinger*

HarperFestival®
*A Division of* HarperCollins*Publishers*

The dog chased the cat

the bug chased the bee

the squirrel chased the squirrel

and someone's chasing me!

The cat scooted away

off buzzed the bee

the squirrel raced across the grass

and you can't catch me!

Now where's that cat?

Now where's that bee

Now where's that squirrel?
Now you can't find me!

Go, cat, go!

Fly away, bee!

Hurry, squirrel, hurry!
And run away, me!

*The dog caught the cat.*

The bug caught the bee.

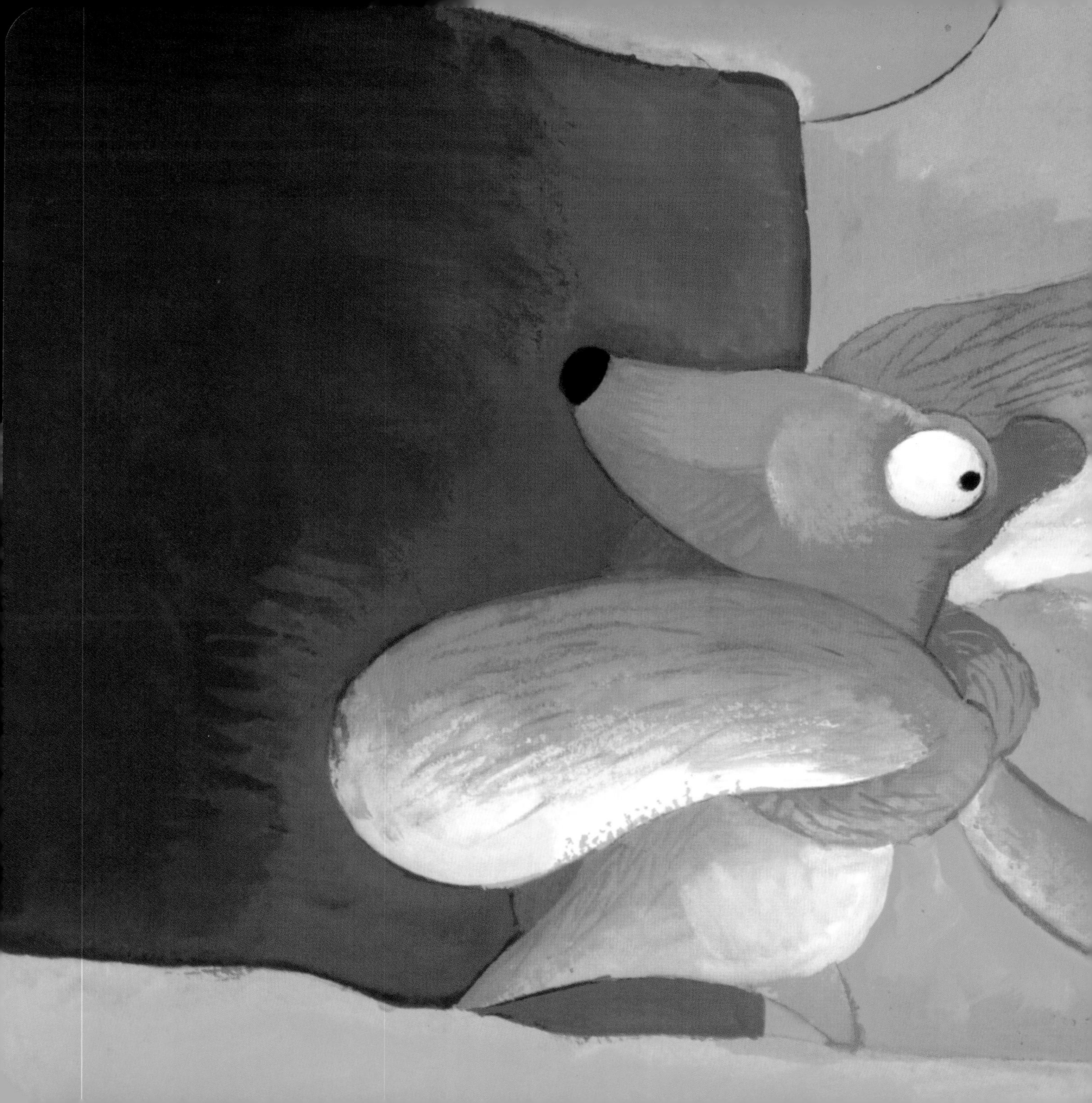

The squirrel caught the squirrel.

But you can't catch me!

You can't catch me!